# HALLOWEEN COSTUME POEM

Printed in the United States of America

ISBN 979-8-89114-242-8 (sc)
ISBN 979-8-89114-243-5 (e)

Library of Congress Control Number: 2025923220

2026.01.08

MainSpring Books
5901 W. Century Blvd
Suite 750
Los Angeles, CA, US, 90045

www.mainspringbooks.com

# Halloween Costume Poem

## Kathleen Whitham

On a sunny fall day,

'Twas October 31,

The costumes were gathered,

Primed up for great fun.

"Which will YOU want to be?"

They all wanted to hear.

"Will you choose to be ME

Trick-or-treating this year?

We know of a game
That might serve as a guide:
"We'll describe who we are,
Then you guess and decide.
Let's get started," they said,
Who will be first to go?"
And then they all lined up
In one Halloween row.

Are you ready to play?
Okay, here is your quiz:
All the costumes will speak—
Can you guess who each is?"

(1)

I ride on a broom,

My nose looks disjointed,

When I laugh I cackle,

My hat's black and pointed,

I hang out with my cat,

Like my hat, black as pitch.

Can you guess who I am?

Yes, you can, I'm a ______!


(2)

My fur is jet black and

My eyes green or yellow;

Some think I'm bad luck but

I'm such a nice fellow.

I meow and I purr

And I might catch a rat.

Do you know what I am?

But of course, a black ______!

(3)

My bed is a coffin,

I'm nothing but bones,

I may try to scare you

With my moans and groans.

I'm so thin my ribs show

And I don't weigh a ton.

Can you guess what I am?

You know, a ______!


(4)

Some think that I'm scary

When I say "boo" and "hoo."

My house may be haunted

But that won't scare you!

I look like a white sheet,

I'm a nice, friendly host:

Come and visit me soon!

Who am I? I'm a ______!

(5)

I bring luck, hope, and joy,

I resemble a horse,

I symbolize freedom

And chase rainbows, of course.

I'm a magical creature

With only one horn,

So you must know by now

That I'm a _______!

(6)

I am small and I squeak

And I like to eat cheese.

I think I'm quite cute,

But some folks I don't please.

My cousin is Mickey;

Can I come to your house?

I'll bring Minnie along.

Guess what I am? A _______!

(7)

If you've been to the circus,

You may have seen me.

I make people happy,

And giggle with glee.

I might have a red nose

And a smile, not a frown,

Orange hair and big feet.

Who am I? I'm a ______!


(8)

I am orange and I'm round,

And my name might be Jack;

I have eyes, nose, and mouth,

But a body I lack.

I will light up at night

If a candle can burn

Inside me. What am I?

I'm a Jack-o'-______!

(9)

My father's the king,

I might wear a pink gown,

I live in a castle,

On my head there's a crown;

To find my prince charming,

I hope for success.

Do you know who I am?

Yes, you do! A _______!

(10)

I'm not so good looking;

I can sometimes be mean,

Or hairy and scary;

I might be blue or green;

But one of my brothers

Would be a good sponsor

For chowing down cookies!

Who's that? Cookie _______!

(11)

I have little horns

And my color is red,

And I tempt you with thoughts

I put into your head,

Like, "Eat candy and sweets,

Sink down to my level."

Of course you say "NO!"

You know me, I'm a _______!

(12)

Skull and crossbones are signs

Of my chosen profession;

I make some walk the plank,

I must make this confession.

Captain Hook and Blackbeard

Are two well-known tyrants

Of the high seas like me.

Now you know we are _______!

(13)

My truck has a siren.

I am strong, fit, and brave;

Burning buildings I enter

When lives are to save.

I douse flames with water

So flames won't burn brighter.

Who am I? You know this!

I'm a proud fire ______!

(14)

Over buildings I bound,

I have power and speed

And I have X-ray vision—

What more could I need?

On my chest there's an S,

Without fail, I've a plan.

You might see me in films.

What's my name? ______!


(15)

I'm a girl, I'm heroic,

I'm strong and I'm daring,

I can fly, I can heal,

I'm kind and I'm caring;

I like talking to all,

Both animal and human.

Can you guess who I am?

Of course! Wonder ______!

All the costumes agreed:

"You're so good at this game!

After every description,

You called each by name.

So what's your decision?

What's your costume this year?

Is it one we have mentioned,

Or another not here?

But whatever you choose

At the end of this rhyme,

You're sure to look great

And you'll have great time!


It's so fun to pretend

To be somebody new,

But the best is beneath

The disguise—AWESOME YOU!


Have the best Halloween ever!

Here are the answers:

1.  Witch
2.  Cat
3.  Skeleton
4.  Ghost
5.  Unicorn
6.  Mouse
7.  Clown
8.  Lantern
9.  Princess
10. Monster
11. Devil
12. Pirates
13. Fighter
14. Superman
15. Woman

# About the Author

Kathleen, a graduate of Indiana University with a master's degree from the University of North Carolina, was a French teacher with over forty years of experience. She is presently the owner and chief chef of a pie- and pastry-making making business in Hillsborough, North Carolina. However, she considers her role as mother of five sons and grandmother of eight to be the role of utmost importance in her life. She has written a number of stories and poems for her grandchildren over the past several years. Three of the books she wrote for them have been published (themes: Thanksgiving, Christmas, and Easter) and this book (featuring Halloween) is the next in the "holiday books for children" series. She hopes you and the children in your life enjoy this one as much as she enjoyed creating it.